P9-EMG-425

For Shaun, with even more love —Avi

Atheneum Books for Young Readers
An imprint of Simon & Schuster
Children's Publishing Division
1230 Avenue of the Americas
New York, New York 10020
Text copyright © 1970 by Avi Wortis
Text copyright renewed © 1998 by Avi Wortis
This compilation copyright © 2002 by Avi
Illustrations copyright © 2002 by Marjorie Priceman
All rights reserved, including the right of
reproduction in whole or in part in any form.
Book design by Lee Wade and Anne Scatto
The text for this book is set in Aunt Mildred.
The illustrations for this book are
rendered in gouache on paper.
Printed in Hong Kong
First Edition
10 9 8 7 6 5 4 3 2 1
Library of Congress Cataloging-in-Publication Data
Avi, 1937–
Things that sometimes happen / by Avi ;
illustrated by Marjorie Priceman.
p. cm.
"An Anne Schwartz book."
Summary: A collection of brief stories including such
titles as "The Hippopotamus's Car," "The Melting Ice-
Cream Cone," and "The Black Crayon."
ISBN 0-689-83914-6
[1. Short stories.] I. Priceman, Marjorie, ill. II. Title.
PZ7.A953 Th 2001
[E]—dc21
00-062043

VERY SHORT STORIES FOR LITTLE LISTENERS

Things that Sometimes Happen

by AVI

pictures by Marjorie Priceman

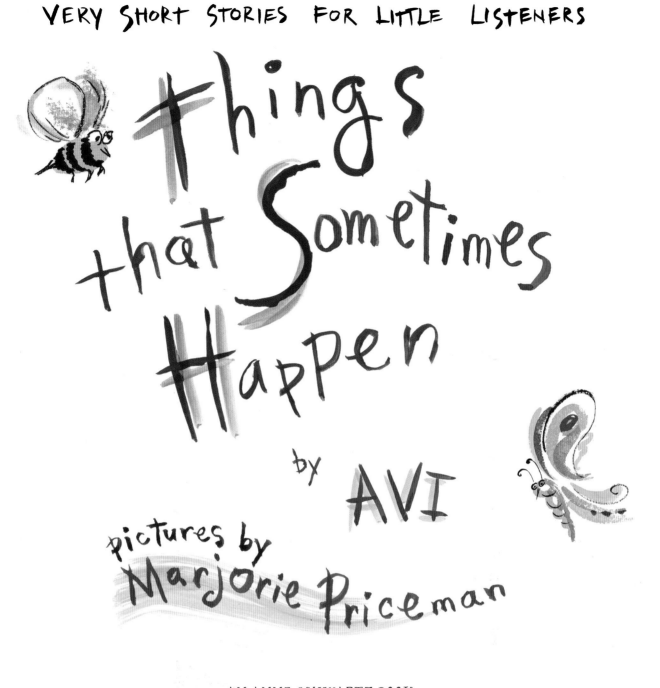

AN ANNE SCHWARTZ BOOK
Atheneum Books for Young Readers
New York   London   Toronto   Sydney   Singapore

A Little Boy came home for lunch and said to his Cat, "Guess where I was. I went to the North Pole. If you don't believe me, look how dirty my shoes are. It's dirty at the North Pole."

His Cat said, "I am sorry you were gone. While you were at the North Pole, a camel came. If you don't believe me, look at my water bowl. It's all empty because the camel drank it."

The Little Boy said, "Guess where else
I was. I went out West, looking for tigers.
If you don't believe me, look how dirty
my hands are. It's dirty work,
looking for tigers."

The Cat said, "Oh,
sorry you were gone.
While you were
chasing tigers, a
dragon came and
ate all my food.

"If you don't believe me, look at my empty food bowl."

Then the Little Boy said, "Guess where else
I was. I almost caught an elephant. Just see
how dirty my face is. It's dirty work
trying to catch elephants."

The Cat said, "Dear, dear.
While you were catching elephants, a
hundred monkeys came. If you don't believe
me, just look how well-combed my fur is. Monkeys comb
fur very well, you know."

Then the Little Boy said, "I also went to the park today."
And the Cat said, "I also slept this morning."

And those are things that sometimes happen.

The Story of the Glass of Water and the Elephant

A Glass of Water was walking along very carefully. He did not wish to spill the water or lose the straw that was stuck in him.

"I do wish," the Glass of Water said to himself, "I do wish somebody would drink me. A Glass of Water needs to have somebody to drink the water or it is no good."

Just then the Glass of Water met a thirsty Elephant.

"Would you please drink me?" said the Glass of Water to the Elephant.

"I would be glad to," said the Elephant. "I am very thirsty." But when he tried to put his trunk into the Glass, the Glass was too small.

"Oh dear," said the Glass of Water. Then the Elephant tried to use the straw. But when he put his trunk over the straw and began to suck, the straw went up his nose.

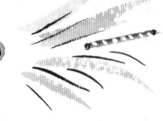

"Oh dear," said the Glass of Water. The Elephant blew out the straw.

Then the Elephant tried to pick up the Glass of Water with his feet, but he could not reach his mouth.

"Oh dear," said the Glass of Water.

"I have an idea," said the Elephant. "I'll stand on my head. Then you can pour water right into my mouth."

The Elephant stood on his head, and the Glass of Water poured himself into the Elephant's mouth. The Elephant drank all the water.

The empty Glass was

very,

very

happy,

and he ran all the way home.

The Hippopotamus's Car

A Hippopotamus wanted to buy a car. It had to be a beautiful car because the Hippopotamus thought that he was very beautiful and he had to have beautiful things around him all the time.

"Please show me your perfectly beautiful cars," said the Hippopotamus to the Man who was selling cars.

"Please come this way," said the Man. "How about this one?" he asked.

The Hippopotamus looked it over and tried to get into the seat.

He could not get past the door.

"I'm sorry," said the Hippopotamus, "it's not a beautiful car."

"How about this one?" said the Man. The Hippopotamus tried to get in, but he could not fit on the seat. "Why, this is not a pretty car either," said the Hippopotamus.

"And this one?" said the Man. But the Hippopotamus could not fit into that one either, and he said,

"That's the ugliest one of all."

Finally the Man had
an idea. He showed the Hippopotamus an
enormous garbage truck. The Hippopotamus fit
through the door. He fit right into the seat. He fit very
well indeed. "Why," he said, "this car is a work of art—the
most beautiful car in the world. And he bought it right
then and there. Off he drove in his special,
beautiful, Hippopotamus's car.

Small Between the Rain

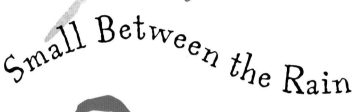

Once upon a time it was raining. A Mama said, "Oh dear. It's raining, and I do need to buy a loaf of bread."

When her Little Boy heard that, he said, "I'll make myself so small, I will run between the raindrops and not get wet at all. Then you can have your bread."

"Do you really think you can?"

"Yes, I am sure I can," said the Little Boy. The Little Boy made himself very small.

Quickly he ran outside. Just as he ran, he was almost hit by a raindrop, but it did miss. He made himself even smaller, and he ran between all the rain. By the time he reached the store he had not gotten wet at all.

At the store he bought some bread.

Home again, home again, he
went, skipping, jumping, turning,
running, never getting hit by the rain.
But just as he missed the very last raindrop—

splash!

He landed in a puddle and got all wet.

"Oh dear," said his Mama. "You got the bread, but you
also got all wet."

"I missed the rain," the Little Boy said, "but I
stepped in a puddle."

"Oh dear."

"Next time," said the Little Boy,
"I'll put on my boots.
Then I won't get
wet at all."

The Black Crayon

A Black Crayon was feeling very unhappy because nobody used him very much. All the other crayons, the red crayon, the blue crayon, all the different ones, were getting shorter and shorter. But the Black crayon was staying very much the same size. "I am just as pretty as the rest," he said to himself.

One day, while a Little Girl was drawing some pictures, he said to her, "I wish sometimes you would use me!"

LIBERTY SCHOOL LIBRARY
ORLAND PARK, ILLINOIS

"I would like to," said the Little Girl,
"but I don't know what to draw."

"Draw a picture of stars, and a moon, and the nighttime, when it's cozy and snug," said the Black Crayon. The Little Girl drew an enormous picture of the nighttime. She put in one, two, three, four, five, six, seven stars. They were yellow and orange. Then she drew a moon. It was purple because she liked purple moons. In fact, she liked the purple moon so much, she made an extra, baby moon. Then everything else she made nighttime, using the Black Crayon to make it lovely dark. When she was all finished it was such a beautiful picture, the Little Girl's Mama put it on the wall.

The Black Crayon was very short and very happy.

Going to Work

One day, after breakfast, a Papa said to his Little Boy, "I don't think I'll go to work today. I have a little cold. Do you think you could take my place?"

"Of course I can," said the Little Boy.

After his Mama had made him a lunch, the Little Boy went to work. When he got to work, he sat at a desk and said yes and no to a lot of people. Then he picked up a telephone and spoke to some more people. Then he looked at some papers. Every once in a while he had some coffee. During the afternoon he called his Mama on the telephone. "How is Papa doing?" he asked.

"Oh, fine," said his Mama. "I think he'll be able to go to work tomorrow."

"Very good," said the Little Boy. "Give him a kiss for me."

When he came home from work, the Little Boy sat on his Papa's bed. "How are you feeling?" he said to his Papa.
"Much better," said Papa.

"I brought you a present," said the Little Boy. And he gave his Papa a book to read. It had no pictures.

The next morning the Papa was feeling much better and he went to work himself.

The Melting Ice-Cream Cone

Once upon a time it was a very hot day. It was so hot that an Ice-Cream Cone was melting because no one was eating him. He ran very fast until he found a large flower, under which it was much cooler. In the shade he did not melt so fast, but drip, drip, he still did melt.

Two Bears came walking along.

"Hurry!" cried the Ice-Cream Cone. "I need you to eat me up because it's too hot and I'm melting."

As he spoke he melted, drip, drip.

"Fine," said the Bears.

"But I get the first lick," said one Bear.

The Ice-Cream Cone went drip, drip.

"No, I get the first lick," said the other Bear.

The Ice-Cream Cone went drip, drip.

The Bears argued and argued. Finally, when they could not make up their minds, they turned to the Ice-Cream Cone and said, "Mr. Ice-Cream Cone, you decide who gets the first lick." But the Ice-Cream Cone was not there. He had melted all away.

Tunnels

Some children were digging in the sandpile. "Let's dig a tunnel home," said a Small Girl.

"I've already started," said another.

They worked very hard, digging, digging, digging, until they made a tunnel. When they came out at the other end, they found themselves in China.

Oh-oh, that was a mistake.

They dug and dug, and when they came out
they found themselves in the middle of an ocean.

Oh-oh, that was a mistake.

They dug, and dug,
and when they came out they found
themselves on top of the Empire
State Building.

Oh-oh, that was a mistake.

They dug, and dug, and when they came out they found themselves at the North Pole.

Oh-oh, that was a mistake. They dug and dug, until finally, they came out right in their own house. Which was a good thing because it was time for ...

lunch.

A Story About a Story

Once upon a time there was a Story that just did not know how to end. It was really a very nice Story, with lots of interesting things to say, even funny things. It went on and on, with all sorts of things happening. But it just could not stop. It tried and it tried, and just when it was going to stop, it thought of something else to say.

"I think," said a

Little Boy who was listening to the Story, "I think the best way to end a story is to say, 'They all lived happily ever after.'"

"Oh no," said a Little Girl with pigtails. "You should end every story with some crying."

Another Little Boy said, "It should end with everybody crying and laughing at the same time."

Another Small Boy said, " A story should end, 'Ha-ha, I told you so.'"

Just then a very old Mouse came along. He had long gray whiskers and a cane. He had listened to many, many stories for many, many years.

In a very squeaky voice the old Mouse said, "The way to end stories is to say, 'The End.' And that is the end." And sure enough,

there wasn't anymore, except

The End.